To, dear Joel,
with lots of love,
from, Grandma and Grandad.
Christmas 1994
x

Based on The Railway Series by The Rev W Awdry

Written by Jenny Lewis

Cover illustration by Owain Bell

Endpaper illustration by Owain Bell

Photographic Stills by David Mitton and Terry Permane for Britt Allcroft's production of "Thomas the Tank Engine & Friends"

Line work and full colour illustrations by David Palmer (Temple Rogers)

Published by
Grandreams Limited
Jadwin House,
205/211 Kentish Town Road,
London, NW5 2JU.

Printed in Italy.

Contents

Good day, friends of Thomas. I thought I would say hello to you all in this year's Thomas and Friends Annual. You mightn't know my true name is Sir Topham Hatt, but I really don't mind everyone calling me The Fat Controller.

As usual, at this time of year, there was quite a commotion in the engine sheds between the engines and trucks as to who should take the honour of introducing this fine book. As you know, I am a fair man and so, to stop any argument, I decided to undertake the task myself.

And it is with great pleasure, that I can introduce to you, stories involving, amongst others, Thomas, one of the most useful engines on my railway, and Oliver, who was rescued from the doom of the scrap heap. Curious as ever, Oliver is continually finding out about our Island of Sodor railway. With the help of Thomas, Oliver learns the excitement of the 5th of November in his story.

As well as reading the stories, there's fun to be had with games and puzzles. So enjoy yourselves!

Easter Egg Special

It was nearly Easter and the children were looking forward to the Grand Easter Egg Hunt on Easter Saturday. James the red engine was feeling very proud that he had been chosen to pull the Easter Egg train.

Saturday morning arrived and James' coaches had been decorated with ribbons and balloons and looked very cheerful indeed. All the children cheered as James pulled into the station to collect the children. The Fat Controller handed each child a map and a sheet of clues to help them find the eggs.

The first clue was a picture of a bluebird and James stopped near the *Bluebird* cafe. The children rushed into the cafe and found eggs in the most unusual places - in tea cups, in sugar bowls and even in the ring of a doughnut.

The second clue was a picture of a horse munching on hay in a hay net and

James stopped near a barn by the line. Inside the barn was a haystack and soon all the children were rumaging in the hay and found lots of brightly painted eggs.

The last stop was back at the station and the clue puzzled the children. It was a riddle:

My first is in Coal but not in Fire,

My second is in Arch but not in Wheel,

My last is in Bertie and also in Bus,

Where are the eggs hidden?

The children searched all over the station, James knew where the eggs were hidden and chuckled to himself. At last, one child climbed up into James' cab and found a large basket full of eggs.

James gave a loud Peep Peep of delight. It had been a spendid day and he was glad that he had been a really useful engine by hiding the last basket of eggs.

Can you find these birds and animals around Mrs Kyndley's cottage?

HEDGEHOG	FOX	DOG	OWL	MOLE
RABBIT	ROBIN	MOUSE	SQUIRREL	GULL
BADGER	CAT	PIGEON	COW	SWALLOW

Can you find the words below?
They appear up, down, side to side and diagonally.

BILL	DUCK	LOCOMOTIVE	SOOT
BLOW	EDWARD	LUGGAGE	STEAM
BOCO	FAT CONTROLLER	MAIN STATION	THOMAS
BOGIE	FUNNEL	OIL	TOOT
CAB	GRADIENT	PLATFORM	TRACTOR
COAL	GUARD	ROD	TRAM
DAISY	HAROLD	SHOVEL	VALVE
DIESEL	LAMP	SLEEPER	WAGONS
DONALD	LOAD	SMOKE	WHISTLE

S	S	N	O	G	A	W	H	I	S	T	L	E
D	O	N	A	L	D	G	U	A	R	D	E	B
P	A	O	L	O	C	O	M	O	T	I	V	E
L	M	I	T	A	T	R	E	P	E	E	L	S
A	B	T	S	A	M	O	H	T	W	S	A	J
T	R	A	M	Y	D	P	A	B	T	E	V	G
F	A	T	C	O	N	T	R	O	L	L	E	R
O	U	S	R	E	I	G	O	B	U	O	D	A
R	M	N	P	A	E	T	L	O	G	A	W	D
M	A	I	N	K	C	R	D	C	G	K	A	I
B	E	A	O	E	L	T	A	O	A	C	R	E
A	T	M	K	I	L	A	O	C	G	U	D	N
C	S	H	O	V	E	L	L	R	E	D	U	T

ANSWERS ON PAGES 44 AND 45

Duck, Diesel and Percy

Each summer on the island of Sodor, a special Picnic Train ride was organised for visitors to the island. The Fat Controller was busy working out which engine would be free to take the Picnic Train.

At the engine shed that morning, the engines were waiting patiently for the Fat Controller to tell them which engine had been chosen.

"I do hope it's me," said Thomas to Percy. "Annie and Clarabel will have such fun showing the visitors all the splendid countryside."

The Fat Controller arrived. "I have decided that Gordon will take the Picnic Train," he announced.

"Oh, Annie and Clarabel will be disappointed," sighed Thomas sadly. As they got older, Thomas' two loyal carriages huffed and puffed a little, but they did still enjoy the holiday outing as much as ever.

Gordon did not look happy. "I am the biggest and fastest engine on the whole railway and I am far too important to take the Picnic Train," he complained angrily.

"Engines on my railway must do as they are told," the Fat Controller told Gordon sternly. "Now go and collect your coaches and take them to the harbour station where

Picnic Express

the visitors will be waiting."

The waiting passengers cheered and waved as Gordon drew into the platform. "I'll show them what a ride on the fastest engine on the whole railway is like," Gordon muttered to himself.

The guard blew his whistle and they were off. Gordon started with such a jerk that his driver fell off balance and knocked the brake off. Gordon rushed on with a loud "WHEESH!" Through the tunnel he raced on past the beautiful Sodor countryside. By the time the driver had managed to slow Gordon down, they were half way round their trip.

The passengers were very angry indeed. When they pulled into the next station, they all got off and started to complain bitterly to the Fat Controller who had just arrived at the station. "Gordon went so fast, we couldn't see any of the countryside," they complained.

"Please Sir," called Thomas, who had pulled in at the other platform. "We can take the visitors at a more leisurely pace."

"Yes, indeed you can Thomas," replied the Fat Controller gratefully. All the passengers climbed aboard Annie and Clarabel and Thomas set off cheerfully. Whenever they passed an especially beautiful part of the island, Thomas slowed down so that everyone got a good view. All the visitors had a lovely ride and they all went home very happy.

Later that evening, Thomas returned wearily to the shed. "What a super day it turned out to be," he thought to himself.

Gordon was still sulking. "Gordon's Picnic Express may have been the fastest, but it certainly wasn't the best," Thomas cheekily announced.

Gordon pretended he hadn't heard.

Thomas is anxious to leave, but four people want to catch him. Can you help them through the maze and find out who gets to Thomas in time?

ANSWERS ON PAGES 44 AND 45

Join the dots

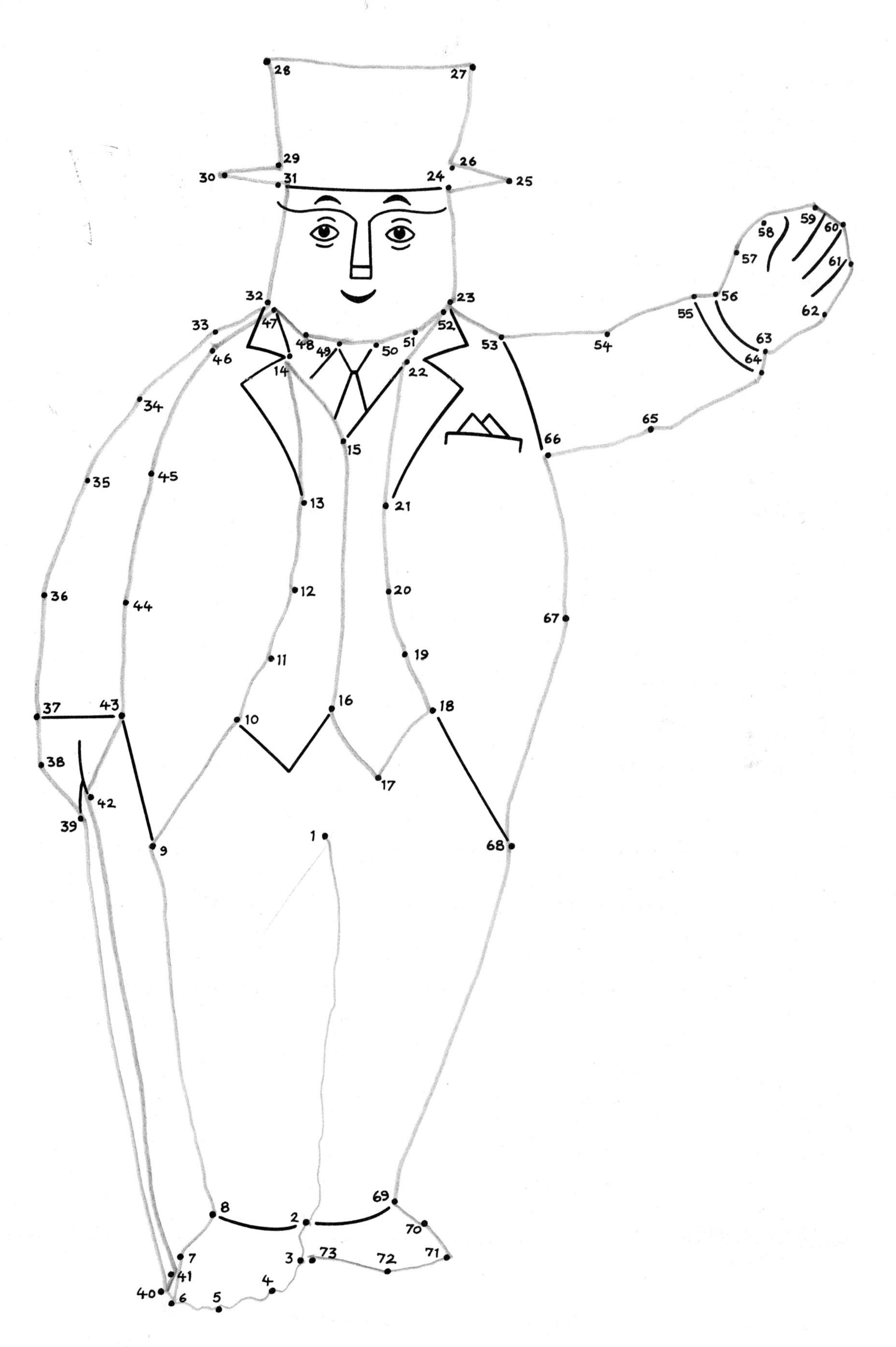

Toby and the Troublesome Trucks

Oliver's Sparkler

One day in early autumn, Oliver noticed a pile of wood in the field next to his branch line. It wasn't doing anything much - just sitting there! The next day, the pile had grown larger. And the day after that it was larger still. On top of the branches and sticks of wood, someone had put an old, broken chair.

At last, Oliver could contain his curiosity no longer and asked his driver if he knew what the mysterious pile of wood was for. His driver laughed, "Well you know what day it is tomorrow Oliver, don't you? It's November the 5th!"

"November 5th? What's so special about November the 5th?" Oliver asked. His driver told him to wait until the next day to find out. The next day came, and Oliver and Thomas found themselves

being loaded up with huge bags of potatoes, and pack after pack of bread rolls and sausages along with several large, brightly coloured boxes. Oliver asked Thomas if he knew what was going on. Thomas knew that November the 5th was fireworks night, and that there would be a big bonfire party in the field next to Oliver's branch line, but he didn't want to spoil the surprise for Oliver. So he just smiled and said, "It's a surprise! But I think whatever it is, it will bring a sparkle to your eyes!"

Later that day, as he pulled into the station, Oliver saw a crowd of people wearing woolly hats, scarves and gloves, all talking excitedly about going to the field where the bonfire was. He heard a little girl asking,

"I hope you've remembered the sparklers Mummy?"

Oliver's driver saw that Oliver couldn't wait any longer to find out what the secret was. "Come on then Oliver, let's go to the bonfire party!" he said.

Oliver stopped in a siding near the field where the bonfire was now brightly burning. Flames leapt into the air, and the people all crowded round with rosy faces lit up by the warm glow. Suddenly there was a BANG...CRASH...SWISHHHH! A stream of light shot into the air and exploded into a mass of

coloured stars. Then another one went off. Then another. Oliver looked on in amazement. He was enjoying his first firework display very much.

A bit later on, some people noticed Oliver and his driver watching, and brought them over a hot potato and a sausage and best of all...a SPARKLER! Oliver thought the sparkler looked just like a magic wand. At last he understood what Thomas meant when he said the surprise would bring a sparkle to his eyes!

Smoke Trail

Follow the smoke trail to catch Thomas. You will need a dice and some counters. Throw the dice and move the number of smoke clouds shown. The first player to Thomas wins the game.

23
24
Finish
Stop to take on water. Go back to 18.
22
13
Children playing near crossing. Go back to 12.
12
11
10
Mrs Kyndley has been forgotten. Go back to 8.
6
7
Bertie stuck on level crossing. Miss a turn.
8
9

Percy and Thomas

Thank You Thomas

Several of the main roads on the Island of Sodor were being repaired. There were big ROAD CLOSED signs and machines digging up the surface of the road and moving piles of stones and earth around. Notices with arrows were set up showing cars that they had take a different route. Quite a few people found it difficult to get to work in the morning and home again at night. To help out, the Fat Controller arranged for Thomas and Toby to run extra train services until people could use the roads again.

It meant a lot of hard work for the two engines, but they were happy to help and

And Toby

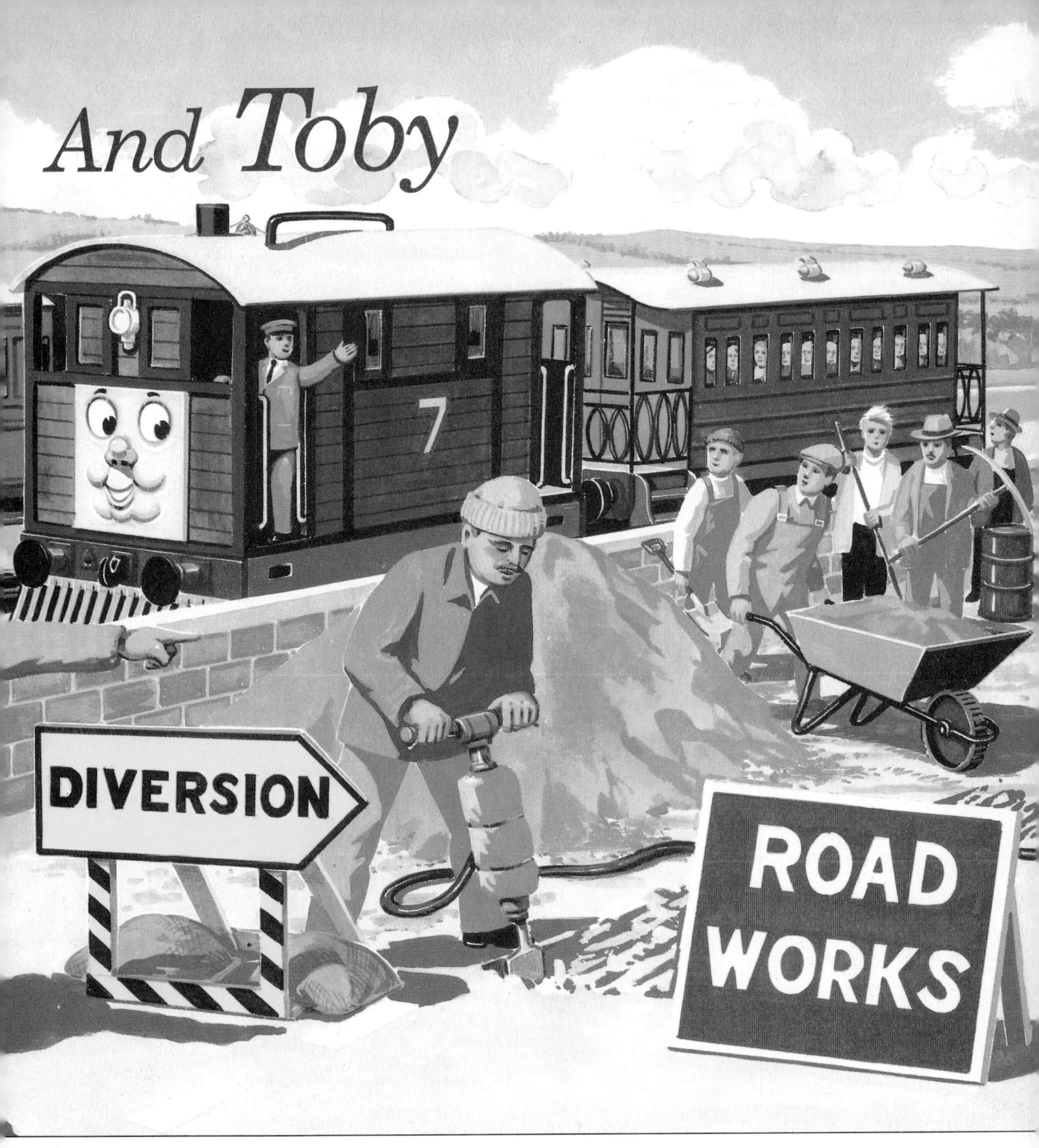

always appeared cheerful and smiling every morning to take on their extra duties.

However cold and wet the day, Thomas and Toby always chuffed along with a warm, friendly welcome for everyone. The extra passengers were so grateful that when the roadworks were finished, they decided to throw a party for the railway staff at the church hall.

Again, Thomas and Toby were kept busy, this time taking bunting, balloons and banners along to the station near to where the party was being held. There was also lots of delicious food. There was jelly and ice cream for the children and Mrs Kyndley had

Thank you
Thomas & Toby

made one of her special cakes. It looked as though it would be great fun but Thomas and Toby were feeling sad as they went home later that evening. They wished they could go to the party too!

When they arrived back at the engine sheds, all the lights were out and everything was quiet. "Goodnight Thomas," Toby said, "I'm not going to think about parties." Thomas replied, "And neither will I Toby, goodnight."

They were about to settle down to sleep when suddenly, all the lights went on. SURPRISE! The engine shed had been decorated with flags, streamers and balloons and all their friends were there. Across the whole of the engine shed was a huge banner saying THANK YOU THOMAS AND TOBY!

The grateful passengers hadn't forgotten about them after all! Thomas and Toby felt proud and happy. And they felt even more so when the Fat Controller came in to tell them he was very pleased with them. "You have done a lot of extra work and always been your usual, cheerful selves," he said. "You are a credit to the railway and you are both really useful engines."

Which two engines are identical?

ANSWERS ON PAGES 44 AND 45

A picture for you to colour

1st Prize

Trevor the Traction Engine was dozing in the Vicarage Orchard enjoying the late summer sunshine. His driver arrived with a bucket, cloth and polish. "There is a Steam Engine Rally at the Village Agricultural Show and I think that you will win the Best Kept Engine Competition," he said.

When his driver had finished cleaning, Trevor looked splendid with all his brass glistening in the sunshine.

Edward arrived on the line that runs past the bottom of the orchard. "My word Trevor," Edward commented, "don't you look marvellous. I am sure you will win a prize at the show."

Edward was on his way to the station to pick up a trailer full of tables for the fruit and vegetable competitions at the show. He also had to

take a trailer containing two special passengers - two of the farmer's donkeys were going to the show to give rides to the children. "Good luck Trevor," called Edward as he set off for the station.

Not long afterwards, the Vicar came running down the orchard to where Trevor and his driver were getting ready to set off for the show. "We need your help Trevor. Edward has broken down and cannot get to the station to pick up the tables and donkeys for the show," explained the Vicar.

Trevor chuffered off to the station yard where he was hooked up to a trailer full of tables. He set off down a narrow muddy lane that led to the show ground to deliver the tables. Trevor then went back to the station yard for the donkeys. But the donkeys did not want to get into the trailer. "Hurry up," pleaded Trevor. "I'll miss the competition if you carry on being so stubborn."

Trevor's driver had an idea, and he hurried off to find some carrots. "These will do the trick," he said and put the carrots in the trailer. The donkeys saw the carrots and jumped in the trailer straight away.

Trevor set off down the muddy lane again and soon reached the show ground. He caught sight of his reflection in the water as he passed the boating lake and was horrified. "Oh goodness, I'm

covered in mud. I can't enter the competition now!" he cried.

"Never mind," said his driver. "We can help the donkeys give rides to the children instead." And that's exactly what they did.

The next day, back in the orchard, the Vicar came to see Trevor and tied a big red rosette with a 1st in the centre onto his funnel. "This is from the children who think that you are the very best traction engine ever." Trevor was delighted and wore his rosette all day.

Can you spot ten differences between these pictures?

ANSWERS ON PAGES 44 AND 45

Can you find ten mice hidden in this picture?

ANSWERS ON PAGES 44 AND 45

Answers

Page 12
Mrs Kyndley's Cottage

Page 20
Maze

Page 13
Word Search

S	S	N	O	G	A	W	H	I	S	T	L	E
D	O	N	A	L	D	G	U	A	R	D	E	B
P	A	O	L	O	C	O	M	O	T	I	V	E
L	M	I	T	A	T	R	E	P	E	E	L	S
A	B	T	S	A	M	O	H	T	W	S	A	J
T	R	A	M	Y	D	R	A	B	T	E	V	G
F	A	T	C	O	N	T	R	O	L	L	E	R
O	U	S	R	E	I	G	O	B	U	O	D	A
R	M	N	P	A	E	T	L	O	G	A	W	D
M	A	I	N	K	C	R	D	C	G	K	A	I
B	E	A	O	E	L	T	A	O	A	C	R	E
A	T	M	K	I	L	A	O	C	G	U	D	N
C	S	H	O	V	E	L	L	R	E	D	U	T

Page 36
Identical Engines
Numbers 4 and 5 are identical

Page 42 Spot The Difference

Page 43 Find The Mice